Barbro Lindgren & Eva Eriksson

JULIA
Wants a Pet

Translated by Elisabeth Kallick Dyssegaard

 R&S
BOOKS

Stockholm   New York   London   Adelaide   Toronto

First there's the apartment building. There are some trees and a little green grass and gravel and garbage cans. Once in a while, crows sit on the rug rack, and right behind it the hyacinths bloom in the spring.

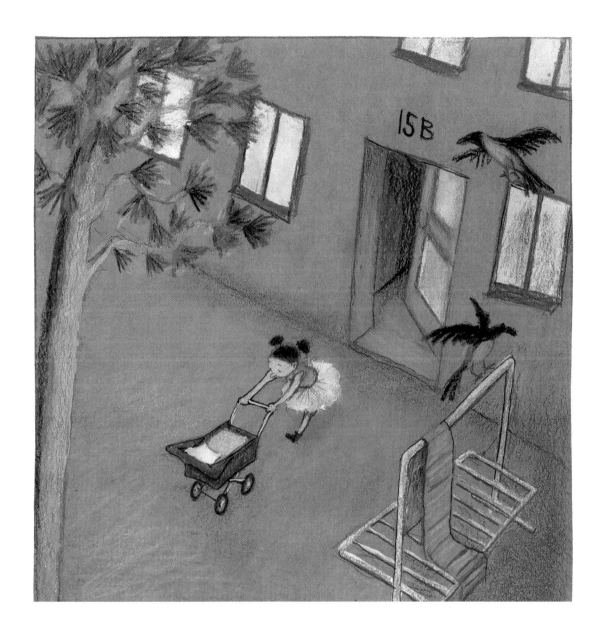

Julia comes racing out of her building with the baby carriage. She's in a big hurry! She's been sitting completely still in the kitchen for a long time. Now she has to run around as much as she can so that her legs won't fall asleep.

Grownups who come into the courtyard look at the rug rack and the garbage cans and say, "It's so ugly here!"

But Julia thinks it's lovely. It's her home. Childhood homes are always lovely. The trees are very tall and the buildings remind her of an Advent calendar, especially in the evening, when all the windows are lit up.

And there's a rock, almost like a horse, right outside her door. Julia rides on it every day. All the kids in the courtyard take turns on the horse before they really start playing.

But right now Julia's alone and wants to play. She sprints
across the lawn with the baby carriage, its little roof and pillow
bouncing up and down. Julia is out looking for a pet. Every
day she looks for a pet. One that can jump up and lick her and
lie down and sleep in the baby carriage.

Julia has always wanted a pet, but she's never had one. Every morning when she wakes up, she says, "Am I getting a pet today?"

"No, my little sweet pea," says her mom. Her dad doesn't say anything, because he doesn't live there.

Julia would like a pony most of all.

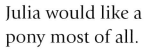

But she would take a hedgehog

or a swan

or a dog.

A rat would be fine, too,

or a big frog.

She doesn't collect worms. They don't even have eyes or legs to jump up with.

Flies are too small—

they're only fun when they need to be buried.

Julia has two beetle graves, a wasp grave, and four fly graves behind the rug rack. Very nice graves, in fact, with crosses that she has made herself.

But today there are not a lot of animals around.
Just two crows hopping about. She tries to catch
the slow one, but just as she's about to grab
hold, it hops away.
And the other
one has flown
off.

In the distance, Julia notices a little boy. She hasn't seen
him before. Perhaps she can squeeze him into the baby
carriage! But he just keeps running around and around.
    "Stop moving!" says Julia.
    "Toot!" he says, continuing to run and jump all over.
    "Why are you jumping?" shouts Julia.
    She's beginning to get pretty mad.

"I'm a steam engine," says the boy. Then he lets out some steam and slows down. There's a lot of squealing when the locomotive brakes.

"What's your name?" asks Julia.

"I don't have a name. Just Engine!"

He jumps and toots and squeals some more.

Julia has to hold on to him so he won't wander off.

"I'm looking for animals that can ride in my carriage," says Julia. "Do you want to help me?"

He seems to want to because he toots several times and chugs along after her.

Where are all the animals? There's not a fly to be seen! At the store down the hill, something wags. A dog's tail!

Then they see the rest of the dog. It is white and brown and all alone. Probably no one cares for it except Julia. What luck and what a sweet dog! Just right for the baby carriage. Only a little bit bigger than Julia's teddy bear.

What if she dressed the dog in the bear's shirt and pants? They're just about the right size.

It would be so much fun! But first she has to free the dog, who's tied up outside the store's entrance. The dog looks very happy and wags its tail.

Engine seems to have forgotten about the dog because he's gone back to driving around and around, tooting like a locomotive.

Julia unfastens the leash and picks up the dog. It's pretty heavy but fits right in the baby carriage. Julia pulls the blankie up over the dog so it can go to sleep. But the dog doesn't want to lie down. It just keeps standing up with the pillow on its head.

"Well, the dog will just have to stand there if it's that dumb," says Julia, heading for home.

But she doesn't get far before she hears a horrible scream.

"What are you doing! Leave my dog alone!"

And a woman snatches the dog.

"It's mine. I found it!" says Julia.

"You leave other people's dogs alone!" says the woman angrily.

The dog looks sad. It probably wanted to keep riding with Julia.

"You can ride another day," Julia whispers to the dog before the woman walks away.

Now Julia doesn't have a dog. But for a little while she did, and it was fun. Who is she going to push in the baby carriage now? When all the dogs and crows and hedgehogs are hiding?

Then Julia gets an idea.

Engine.

Engine isn't exactly an animal, but she can see that he's just the right size for the baby carriage. She only has to press him down properly!

Engine doesn't hear her coming. He's chugging along at full speed.

Julia catches him and stuffs him into the baby carriage.

　He fits perfectly! There's even room for his large head. And when she pulls the roof up over him, he can barely be seen.

Off they go. It doesn't do him any good to scream.
"ENGINE! I'm an engine! Let me out of here!"
But Julia doesn't let him out. He has to lie there and
scream because that's what babies do.

After a while he gets tired of screaming and starts to sound like an engine again.

Julia doesn't think it's fun anymore, so she takes him out of the baby carriage. Red in the face and without a word, Engine chugs on home.

What is Julia supposed to do when there are no babies or animals? She sits down on the stone horse to think. Then she sees something shiny green in the grass, almost like a caramel wrapper.

It's a pretty beetle! Green on the back and black on the stomach, it's alive and wiggling all its legs. She puts it in the baby carriage right away and pulls up the roof so it can sleep.

Julia pushes the baby carriage until the beetle closes its tiny eyes.

It's not as much fun as a dog, but it is something! And later, if it dies, she can bury it next to the other beetles and sing and lay small flowers by the grave.

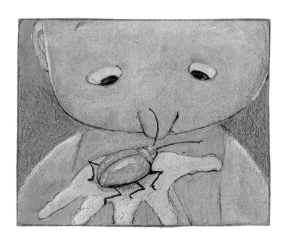

But the beetle doesn't die. It flies away that evening.
Then for her eighth birthday, Julia gets her very own cat!